E.T. and me

SIMON SPOTLIGHT
An imprint of Simon & Schuster Children's Publishing Division
1230 Avenue of the Americas, New York, New York 10020

Manufactured in the United States of America

First Edition
2 4 6 8 10 9 7 5 3

ISBN 0-689-84366-6

E.T. and me

BY KIM OSTROW
BASED ON A MOTION PICTURE
SCREENPLAY
BY MELISSA MATHISON
ILLUSTRATED BY RUDY OBRERO

Simon Spotlight

New York London Toronto Sydney Singapore

CHAPTER 1

Something BIG happened tonight. Something so big, it was out of this world. . . .

It all started when my brother, Mike, and his friends were playing Dungeons & Dragons and having a great time eating chips and drinking soda.

They didn't let me play 'cause it was kind of late and they were in the middle of the game. Mike's friend told me to go wait for the pizza man instead. So I grabbed my baseball mitt and a ball and went outside.

When the pizza man came to our house—which is at the top of a dead-end street, right by a forest—I paid for the pizza and started to run back to the house.

Then . . . *BANG! CRASH!* I heard a loud noise coming from my backyard! I froze for a second and then looked around, but I didn't see a thing. I called for my dog, Harvey. But he didn't come running.

Then I crept around the side of the house. I kept calling for Harvey, but he still wouldn't come.

It was kind of dark in the backyard. And there was this strange mist coming out of the toolshed. It was pretty spooky.

I walked closer and closer to the shed. I was a little nervous, but I threw my baseball into the shed to scare whatever might be in there. I couldn't believe it when the ball came back at me and landed right at my feet! Something was really in there!

I ran back to the house. My heart was beating so fast!

"Help! Let me in!" I screamed until Mom finally opened the door. I was out of breath, and Mike and his friends looked at me like I was a freak.

"There's something out there," I said. But Mike and all his friends just laughed. "I'm telling you," I said really seriously, "nobody go out there."

No one moved for a second, then Mike said, "Let's go!" and everybody ran outside—even Mom.

Everyone looked around the backyard. Then Mike found some weird footprints by the shed, and they all thought it was that dumb coyote that had been in our backyard last year.

"Okay, that's it," Mom said. "Party's over, everyone inside."

We trudged back into the house. I told Mom that there really was something out there. She said she knew, and patted me on the head. She always does that when she doesn't believe me.

I fell asleep that night wondering what could possibly be out there. Suddenly I heard *BANG! CRASH!* again. I jumped out of bed and ran to the backyard.

I guess I was pretty crazy to go looking for something in the middle of the night by myself, but I had to find out. I knew it wasn't just a dumb coyote.

Then I heard a noise that kind of sounded like a big frog. It seemed to be coming from the cornstalks, so I went over there and shined my flashlight around, but I didn't see anything except cornstalks.

And that weird noise was getting louder and louder.

So I shined the flashlight again and suddenly saw something with a big head and two huge eyes and some pointy teeth staring right at me!

I screamed, and the creature

screamed! And then the big head thing ran right past me and straight out of our back gate.

There *was* something out there. And then it was gone!

CHAPTER 2

The next morning I got on my bike to try and follow whatever had been hiding in my backyard.

I knew it wasn't a coyote, so I was determined to figure out what it was. I had a full bag of candy in case I got hungry. I would look all day, if that's what it took.

I rode around in the forest for a while, but couldn't find it. I kept calling, "Hello!" But no one answered.

Then I got this idea . . . I would drop the candy pieces all the way home, like a trail. Maybe whoever it was would find the candy and follow them. It was a brilliant idea (if I do say so myself!).

When I got home I dragged a chair from the shed into the backyard. I decided to plant myself in the chair to wait. I waited all day. Nothing. Then I guess I fell asleep, because the next thing I remember, something odd woke me up. It was that strange frog sound again. I thought I was dreaming.

But when I opened my eyes, I saw that it wasn't a dream! At the edge of the yard stood the strangest-looking creature I had ever seen in my whole life. He—I figured it was a he—was half my size,

with a round body, and he had long skinny arms and funny-looking feet.

"Mom . . . Michael . . . ," I tried to call, but the words couldn't really come out. He started to come closer and I held my breath! He waddled over slowly, making weird frog sounds, and then he stuck out his arm—I didn't know what he was going to do!—and slowly opened his fist. He dropped a handful of the candy pieces onto my blanket! I couldn't believe it! He had followed my trail!

I wanted to bring him into the house right away. So I dropped more candy in the backyard and made another trail all the way up to my room. And the little guy kept picking up the pieces, popping them into his mouth, and eating them! It was so funny. You should have seen how he walked. He kind of waddled from side to side.

Anyway, I finally got him to my room. But he started picking up my toys and then dropping them on the floor. He was making so much noise, I was afraid Mom would wake up and see him—or even worse, my little sister, Gertie, would wake up, freak out, and ruin everything. So I closed my door and locked it. Now it was just him and me.

He was standing under a lamp, and I was staring at him. He was staring back at me when a bizarre thing happened: I scratched my nose, and then he scratched his nose. I pointed to my mouth, and he did the same! I raised my hand and started to wiggle my fingers.

He copied that, too, except he only had four fingers. It was so awesome!

Then his eyelids started to droop. He looked sleepy. And the more tired he looked, the more tired I felt. So I went to sit in my big armchair. The next thing I knew, I was asleep.

CHAPTER 3

There was no way I was going to school the next day! So I faked sick.

Mike taught me this trick once, where you put the thermometer on a lightbulb to make the temperature go up, and it looks like you have a fever. It was the perfect day for that trick. And Mom fell for it! She asked if I had been up all night waiting for that "thing" to come back. I said, "Yeah."

If Mom only knew that the "thing" was right there in my closet! And it wasn't a "thing." I liked to believe that he was some sort of extra-terrestrial creature. So I decided to name him E.T. Get it? E.T. for Extra-Terrestrial?

Anyway, Mom was making sure I was tucked in bed and stuff, and then she went into my closet to get extra blankets. I was freaking out because E.T. was hiding in there.

Mom grabbed this blue blanket, and it was all round and puffy, and I thought E.T. had somehow gotten inside it. When she threw it on me, I was so scared he would fall out! But I didn't need to worry. E.T. was still safe in my closet.

It felt like forever before everyone got

out of the house. Finally it was quiet. I led E.T. out of the closet.

"Do you talk?" I asked him, but he didn't say anything. He kept poking at everything in my room. So I figured he was curious about life on Earth.

I had a can of soda and I told him it was a drink. I showed him my action figures and told him how to play with them.

I brought out my candy dispenser, some change, and a toy car. He tried to eat the car, which made me think he was hungry. I knew I was.

So I opened my bedroom door, and Harvey rushed into my room. He growled and barked like crazy at E.T., who was so scared, he ran back into the closet.

I grabbed Harvey and brought him downstairs. Before I went, I told E.T. to stay where he was.

"I'll be right here," I told him.

Okay, so I went downstairs to try and figure out what an alien from outer space might like for breakfast.

I got some cheese and milk and stuff out of the fridge and was trying to carry it all when suddenly I got scared. I had no idea what scared me. All I knew was that I dropped everything on the floor.

I had a funny feeling my being scared had something to do with E.T., so I ran upstairs to make sure he was okay. He was hiding in the closet like he was scared too!

And I saw my umbrella open in the

middle of my room. Maybe E.T. was playing with it and he got scared when it opened?

It was strange that E.T. and I were both scared at almost the same time.

What did this mean? I needed help figuring it out, but at that point, no one knew about E.T. but me.

CHAPTER 4

I couldn't keep E.T. a secret anymore. I had to tell someone. So I chose Mike. I waited until he got home from school. But I almost changed my mind when he came to my room and said, "How you feeling, faker?"

I was mad, but I told him to swear the most excellent promise he could make, which means pretty serious business in our house. He sort of agreed. But this was too important for him to "sort of agree."

So I told him he had to swear as my brother, swear on our lives. I could tell he was getting mad.

"Okay, okay," he said, "don't get so heavy."

When I told him to take off his football shoulder pads and close his eyes, he said I was pushing it. But he finally did as I said, and I brought out E.T. and told Mike to open his eyes. I think Mike nearly fainted!

And before he had a chance to say a word, Gertie burst into my room. She screamed when she saw E.T., and then E.T. started screaming. And then Mike started screaming!

It was a nightmare. Especially when

I heard Mom come home. I immediately shoved everyone into the closet to hide.

When Mom came into my room, she was shocked at the mess.

"I'm just reorganizing," I said. I couldn't tell her that I had an alien in my room who threw things around!

When she left, I opened the closet door. I told Gertie that E.T. wouldn't hurt her. And then I made her promise not to tell anyone. But that wasn't easy. She wanted to know why. So I said that grown-ups couldn't see him. But she didn't buy that.

So even though I didn't want to, I had to take more serious measures. Mike and I pretended to kidnap her favorite doll, which made Gertie finally promise not to tell. We all promised.

That night E.T. sat in my room, eating more food than you can imagine.

Gertie asked if he was a pig, "'Cause he sure eats like one," she said. She gave E.T. a pot of dead flowers (she can be a little weird sometimes).

Anyway, I decided that it was time to find out for sure where E.T. was from. So I pulled out an atlas, and Mike got a globe. I pointed to the globe and to California.

"I'm from Earth," I told E.T. "Earth. Home. Where are you from?"

E.T. pointed out the window. So I opened the atlas to the page with a picture of the solar system. E.T. picked

up some balls of modeling clay from the table and placed them on the planets on the page.

Then out of nowhere—don't ask me how—E.T. made all the clay balls rise off the page and orbit around one another! We just stood there, staring, with our mouths open.

After a few seconds the table started to shake. And then something made me scream and all the balls fell to the floor. I felt really, really scared for the first time since I found E.T., and I wasn't sure what was making me so scared.

I ran down to the backyard to see if I could find something out there. It was pretty dark outside, but I think I saw the shadow of a man. But I wasn't sure, so I didn't say anything.

And can you believe things got even weirder? When I got back to my room, the pot of flowers that Gertie had brought in was still there, but the flowers weren't dead anymore. They were bright and alive!

I asked E.T. if he did it, and he nodded. E.T. could bring dead flowers back to life! That was incredible.

CHAPTER 5

I finally had to go to school and leave E.T. alone at home. No more faking sick.

In science class we were supposed to dissect frogs. Our teacher was telling us exactly what was supposed to happen. I kept staring at the poor frog in the glass jar and couldn't help thinking of E.T.

I leaned in real close to the jar, staring into the frog's eyes. I asked if it could talk. It just stared back.

Our teacher was going around the room dropping cotton balls dipped in some stuff that would put the frogs to sleep, and I just couldn't take it! When he dropped the cotton into my frog's jar, something made me say, "Save me," and I turned my jar upside down to free my frog.

But I wasn't just going to save my frog. I wanted to set them all free. So I ran around the class, turning every jar over, screaming, "Run for your lives! Back to the forest, to the river," and stuff like that.

I don't know what came over me. It was very, very strange. I guess my teacher thought so too because I ended up in the principal's office.

I came home from school, eager to see E.T., and you would not believe what Gertie did. She dressed E.T. up like a girl! It was totally ridiculous. She put him in a dress, with Mom's curly blond wig—and lipstick! He looked like a fool.

I told Gertie to give him back his dignity, but she didn't care. She thought he looked great.

Then Gertie showed me all these things that E.T. had dragged into my room. There was a record player, an umbrella, her Speak & Spell toy, a toaster, a fork, and some other things he'd found. I couldn't imagine what he needed all that stuff for, but he seemed to really want it.

And then he said, "Elliott."

I was shocked! "You can talk!" I shouted.

Gertie told me that she'd taught E.T. how to talk. I went up to him and said, "E.T."

And he repeated it! Gertie was right—he talked now! I was so surprised, I could barely talk myself.

Then he waddled over to the window, pointed his finger toward the sky, and said, "E.T. home. Phone."

I had no idea what he was talking about, but he was talking! He said it again, "E.T. home. Phone."

Then Gertie said, "E.T. phone home? He wants to call somebody!"

"E.T. phone home?" I asked. And he repeated it. He was saying it over and

over, and then it hit me. "And they will come?" I asked.

"Come," he said.

I had to help E.T. get in touch with his family on his home planet, and they would come get him. But what could I do to help?

CHAPTER 6

Mike and I went into the garage to see if we could find things to help E.T. make some kind of radar machine so he could contact his family. We weren't sure what to look for, but we put a lot of stuff in a box anyway.

While we were collecting stuff, Mike said, "You know, E.T. hasn't been looking too good lately."

That made me mad. "Don't say that!

We're fine!" I said, glaring at Mike.

He looked at me like I was nuts and asked me when I started saying "we" when it came to E.T. I pretended I'd made a mistake and said that I'd meant "he." But that wasn't really true. I had meant "we."

I couldn't explain what I was feeling to Mike. I wasn't sure I could explain it to anyone. Somehow I thought I felt whatever E.T. felt. Like when E.T. was tired, I was tired. When he got scared, I got scared too. I didn't know why or how, I just knew that it was true.

After Mike and I found whatever we could, we brought the box up to E.T. I reached into the box to pull out a round sawblade and cut my finger by mistake.

"Ouch!" I said, and then E.T. said "ouch" too!

What happened next was truly amazing. E.T. pointed his finger toward me, and the tip of his finger started to glow! It looked like he had a mini light-bulb on the end of it. I couldn't believe my eyes!

He pointed his finger at my cut. And then guess what? My cut was healed!

CHAPTER 7

Finally it was Halloween night. I thought it would be the perfect time to get E.T. out of the house without Mom seeing.

Gertie pretended that she was going to dress up as a ghost, instead of the cowgirl she goes as every year, and she could go ahead of us. Then we could dress E.T. up as a ghost and Mom would think it was Gertie.

The plan was for Gertie to go ahead

so she could take my bike to the look-out point near the forest. We'd meet up with her, and then E.T. and I would go to the forest so he could call his planet.

So while Mom was in the shower, Gertie left for the lookout. Then Mike and I came down with E.T. dressed in a white sheet. I was dressed like a hunchback so I could hide the stuff that E.T. needed under my hump.

Mike and I were really nervous, but Mom didn't suspect a thing!

When we got to the lookout, Gertie was there with my bike. Mike told me to be back one hour after sundown. I told him that I'd try but that he'd have to cover for me if I didn't make it back on time. I had no idea how long it would take for E.T. to make a "phone" or to contact his family, but I knew I had to help E.T. no matter what.

I rode my bike to the forest with E.T. all wrapped up in his sheet in the front basket of my bike. I was pedaling pretty fast so we'd have as much time as we could for E.T. to make his call.

When we got to the bumpy, thick part of the forest, I knew we'd have to get off the bike and walk because it was too hard to go fast on the trail.

But I guess E.T. didn't want to walk because somehow, all of a sudden, he raised my bike into the air! We kept going higher and higher above the trees. It was fantastic!

I was pedaling, but I wasn't sure if I

needed to. I have to admit I was nervous about landing and I shouted for E.T. to not let us crash. We both kind of fell off the bike when we landed, but we weren't hurt.

We ran to the "bald spot" of the forest, which is what Mike and I called the clearing. We began to set up the "phone." You should have seen E.T. go. I couldn't believe he could make a phone out of the stuff we found.

E.T. placed the round sawblade on my old record player, then he hooked Gertie's Speak & Spell toy to it with wires. He put a wooden hanger above the sawblade, with wires hanging from it. There were more wires connecting the toy to an old radio.

E.T. tied a string to the arm of the

record player and connected it to a tree branch. Then we just waited.

When the wind started to pick up and the trees started blowing back and forth, the string tightened. Somehow that made all the pieces work together, and the Speak & Spell lit up and started dialing.

I know this sounds unbelievable, but it all really happened. I was right there.

"It's working! You did it!" I shouted.

"Home! Home!" E.T. said.

It was getting late, and there was still no response to E.T.'s phone call. I was sure Mom was getting upset that I hadn't come home with Mike and Gertie.

I told E.T. that we had to go. He just kept saying, "Home." And he looked really sad.

I told him that he should give his family time, that they would call back. But E.T. looked even sadder. "Ouch," he said.

I tried to get E.T. to change his mind and stay on Earth with me. I told him he could be happy and that I would take care of him. I told him we could grow up together. It would be great.

I started to cry and E.T. started to cry. He reached over and touched my face, the way Mom does sometimes. Then he looked up at the sky and said, "Home."

CHAPTER 8

I guess I must have fallen asleep in the forest. When I woke up it was morning, and E.T. was nowhere to be found! I shouted his name a few times, but he never came. I was so cold, I was shivering. I was feeling really sick.

But somehow I managed to ride my bike home. When I got there, a police-man was in my kitchen. Mom had called the police when I didn't come home. She hugged me tighter than she ever had in my whole life and told me never to do that again. She felt my forehead and said that I felt hot.

All I could worry about was where E.T. had disappeared to. When Mom wasn't listening, I told Mike that he had to go find him. I told him to check the clearing in the forest and to hurry.

Mike finally came home with E.T. that night. He had found him lying in a creek. E.T. was gray and really sick, and I felt exactly the same way.

Mike wrapped E.T. in a blanket and laid him on the bathroom floor. We were lying there together, sick. I think Mike was scared to see us so sick, so he decided that he had to tell Mom.

I wasn't sure if I wanted Mom to know, but I was scared for E.T., so I said it was okay.

Mike opened the bathroom door and Mom saw us both lying there. She started to laugh 'cause I think she thought E.T. was a toy or something I had made. But when she saw my face and I said, "We're sick. I think we're dying," she knew I was serious.

She had a look on her face like I had never seen. Mom scooped me up, to get me away from E.T.

Gertie shouted, "He won't hurt you, he's the man from the moon!"

I screamed that E.T. shouldn't be left alone, but Mom didn't want to hear it. She wanted to get us out of

the house as fast as possible.

Things started to get even worse after that. Mom opened the door to take me to the hospital, and she came face-to-face with men dressed in space suits. You could hear their heavy breathing through their helmets, and it was terrifying. These guys ran past us, straight to the bathroom, where they grabbed E.T.

There was no way I could stop them— but what were they going to do to E.T.?

CHAPTER 9

There were scientists and doctors all over the house. Our house was even wrapped in thick plastic! They told us that no one was allowed into or out of the house. Then they brought E.T. and me into this lab they had made right in the living room.

The doctors hooked us up to machines, and to each other, to monitor us. It was awful.

They asked me a lot of questions, poked us, and even stuck us with some needles to take our blood.

E.T. was making horrible sounds and I was crying. I was screaming to the doctors that they had no right to do this, that E.T. had come to me.

Then this doctor came over. His voice was very calm and he said, "He came to me, too."

He told me that he had wished for something like this to happen since he was ten years old. I wasn't sure what he was talking about, but he seemed like the nicest doctor of the bunch. He leaned in close and asked me what they could do for E.T.

"E.T. has to go home," I said. The doctor said that E.T.'s arrival was a miracle.

And that he was glad he came to me first. I was too.

And then E.T. took a turn for the worse. He started wheezing. The funny thing was, the worse E.T. got, the stronger and better I felt.

I shouted to him, "I'll be right here!"

But it was too late. E.T. had stopped breathing.

The doctor asked if I wanted to spend a little time alone with E.T. before they took him away. I told him yes!

E.T. was wrapped in plastic and lying in ice in this machine. It was so sad to see him like that. I couldn't believe what they had done to him. I leaned over and told E.T. that I would believe in him for the rest of my life.

"I love you, E.T.," I said. Then I started to walk away.

But then I saw something really peculiar. When I came in to talk to E.T., I saw that Gertie's flowers were on the table, and that they were dead. But now they were alive! You know what that meant?

I ran over to E.T. I could see his heart through his skin and it had started to glow a bright red. That's when his eyes opened and he shouted, "E.T. phone home! E.T. phone home!"

E.T. was alive!

CHAPTER 10

I came up with another excellent plan. Even though I wanted more than anything to have E.T. stay with me, I knew that I had to get him to his home. I didn't want doctors running any more tests on him.

I knew that the only way to get E.T. out was to keep his being alive a secret. So I only told Mike. And I asked him for help. I made him sneak into the van that was supposed to take E.T. away. Then I made a big stink to the doctor about needing to stay with E.T. I pretended to cry, so they let me get into the van with E.T. in his machine. Then Mike took off, even though he could barely drive!

We stopped on the way to tell Mike's friends to take our bikes and meet us in the forest. When the truck got as far as it could in the forest, we jumped out and got on our bikes.

I put E.T. in my bike basket again and we pedaled fast. Suddenly we were being chased by a pack of black cars, so we took a shortcut. And when a few cars finally managed to corner us, guess what E.T. did? He lifted all of us, on our bikes, into the air again! You should have seen the looks on the faces of Mike and his friends!

When we finally got to the clearing, we saw a really bright light coming from the sky. The wind was blowing like crazy.

Then a spaceship landed in front of our eyes!

Mom and Gertie and that nice doctor got to the spot just in time. I had written a note for Gertie to give to Mom, explaining what we were doing.

Gertie ran over to E.T with the pot of flowers. She handed it to him and kissed his nose. "Be good," he told her.

Mike gave E.T a hug. "Thank you," E.T. said.

Then I went up to E.T. "Come?" he asked.

But I shook my head and told him I

had to stay. That was one of the hardest things I've ever had to do.

"Ouch," said E.T.

We hugged good-bye. Then he pointed his finger at my forehead and said, "I'll be right here."

E.T. looked at all of us one more time before climbing up the ramp of his spaceship. We watched the door close, and the last thing I saw was the red glow in E.T.'s chest.

The spaceship took off and actually made a rainbow appear in the sky. E.T was on his way home.

You know, even though I wish E.T. could have stayed to grow up with me and live in my room forever, I know deep down it's better that he was back in outer space with his family.

I am the luckiest kid in the world to have met and become friends with him. And I know that for the rest of my life E.T. will always be right here, in my head and in my heart.

And that's good enough for me.

BE AN *E.T.* TORCHBEARER.

2002 marks the 20th anniversary of E.T. The Extra-Terrestrial. During this time of celebration, E.T. will carry the torch for Special Olympics. Here are some ways you can help too...

 Be a friend to a person with mental disabilities. E.T. and Elliott didn't let differences stand in the way of friendship. Follow their example by spending time with someone with mental disabilities, learning about their challenges and what they like to do.

 Become a fan of a Special Olympics athlete or team. Cheer for Special Olympics athletes at local competitions. Make posters to hang at school to let everyone know that your friends will be going for the gold.

 Rid the world of "Retard." Stop calling people "retard" and encourage your friends to stop saying that hurtful and disrespectful word.

 Label them Able. Everyone has different levels of abilities. Recognize people for what they can do, not for what they can't do.

Visit the E.T. 20th Anniversary Web site (www.et20.com) or the Special Olympics Web site (www.specialolympics.org) to learn more great things about the E.T.-Special Olympics partnership.